If you hold my hand

Written by Jillian Harker
Illustrated by Andy Everitt-Stewart

Bright ☆ Sparks

Oakey's mom opened the front door. "Come on, Oakey. Let's go outside and explore."

But Oakey wasn't really sure. He was only small, and the world looked big and scary.

"Only if you promise to hold my hand," said Oakey.

So Oakey's mom led him down the long lane.
Oakey wished he was back home again!

"This looks like a great place to play. Shall we take a look? What do you say?" asked Oakey's mom.

"Only if you hold my hand," said Oakey.

And Oakey did it!

"Look at **me**! I can do it!" he cried.

"This slide looks like fun. Would you like to try?" asked Oakey's mom.

Oakey looked at the ladder. It **stretched** right up to the sky.

"I'm only small," said Oakey. "I don't know if I can climb that high—

unless you hold my hand."

And Oakey did it!

"Wheee! Did you see me?" he cried.

"We'll take a shortcut through the woods," said Oakey's mom.

"I'm not sure if we should," said Oakey. "It looks dark in there. Well, I suppose we could—*will you hold my hand*?"

And Oakey did it!

"Boo! I scared you!" he cried.

Deep in the woods,
Oakey found a stream,
shaded by beautiful
tall trees.

"Stepping stones, look!"
said Oakey's mom.
"Do you think you could jump
across these?"

"Maybe," said
Oakey. "*I just need you
to hold my hand, please.*"

And Oakey did it!

One…

two…

three...

four...

"Your turn now, Mom," cried Oakey,
holding out his hand.

Beyond the woods, Oakey and his mom
ran up the hill, and all the way
down to the ocean.

"Come on, Oakey," called his mom.

"Would you like to paddle in the sea with me?"

But the ocean looked **big**, and he was only small.

Suddenly, Oakey
knew that didn't
matter at all.
He turned to
his mom and

smiled...

"I can do **anything** if you hold my hand," he said.